the little people

THE TRAPPS FAMILY ADVENTURES

the little people

By LAWRENCE E. R. ADAMS

Illustrations by ROBERT G. ADAMS

TRAPPS PUBLISHING

THE PUBLISHER:
Trapps Publishing
P.O. Box 212
Irricana, Alberta, Canada T0M 1B0

Library and Archives Canada Cataloguing in Publication

Adams, Lawrence E. R. (Lawrence Edward Roy), 1941-, author
    The little people / by Lawrence E.R. Adams ; illustrations by Robert G. Adams.

(The Trapps family adventures)
Includes index.
ISBN 978-0-9781533-1-1 (pbk.)

    I. Adams, Robert G. (Robert Gordon), 1968-, illustrator
II. Title. III. Series: Adams, Lawrence E. R. (Lawrence Edward Roy), 1941- Trapps family adventures.

PS8601.D454L57 2013   jC813'.6   C2013-904449-3

Cover: Robert G. Adams
Printing: Houghton Boston

DISCLAIMER

All the characters in this book are fictitious; any similarity between any persons living or deceased is merely a coincidence.

For Ty, Payton, Parker, Reese, McKenna and Grayson, our Little People

<u>AWARDS</u>

"THE OLD ONE," the first book in, **"THE TRAPPS FAMILY ADVENTURES,"** series, was awarded the silver medal for Canada-West-Best Regional Fiction at the 12th Annual Independent Publisher Book Awards in Los Angeles on 30th May 2008.

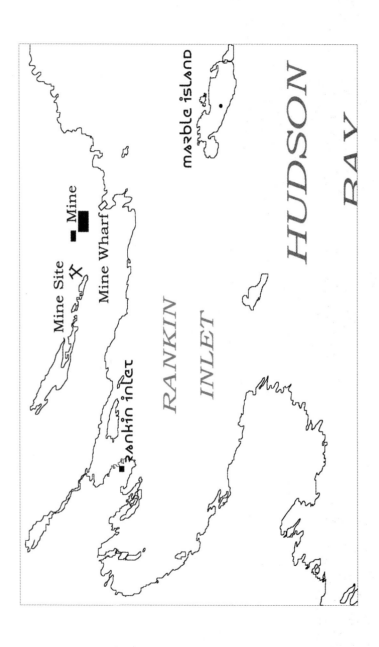

Mine

Mine Site

Mine Wharf

Rankin Inlet

RANKIN

INLET

marble island

HUDSON

BAY

CONTENTS

PROLOGUE 9

GLOSSARY 75

PROLOGUE

It isn't the call of the North that brings the Trapps family to the vast treeless region of Canada known as the Tundra. This trip has nothing to do with the romance "the call of the North" evokes; this isn't even going to be a holiday. Numerous hours of backbreaking work will dominate the expedition, or so they think.

Max Trapps, a world-class archaeologist, has led expeditions to numerous places in the world, conducting excavations to uncover the secrets of the past. Now he's been chosen to conduct an archaeological dig at an ancient Inuit settlement. Workers at the Blue Diamond Mine, approximately thirty kilometres northeast of Rankin Inlet on the west shore of Hudson Bay in the Northwest Territories, made the discovery while working near their airstrip. For the duration of the dig, the mining company will generously supply food and lodgings for the entire Trapps family, which includes Max, his wife Nadine, and their three children.

When Amy, Ty, and Parker meet the Old One, whom the adults know as Kadluk, the secrets and mysteries of the North and the Inuit way of life are laid bare before them in an environment few people have ever seen and even fewer will ever live in. This harsh and unforgiving land holds untold beauty, mystery, and adventure for those who dare to accept its challenges.

The North is home for the Inuit, the only race of humans able to live under its conditions without assistance from the outside world. The Inuit's ability to adapt to their environment allows them to reap the bounty of the North. Only the most adventurous and well-equipped explorers can penetrate the Inuit's habitat and live to tell about it.

Amy's curiosity and her thirst for knowledge sometimes get her into jams that require the help of her brothers to resolve. She enjoys assisting her father during excavations and likes nothing better than discovering a relic from the past and unlocking its secrets.

Ty is twelve, one year younger than Amy, and a gifted athlete. His favorite sport is hockey, and if he were allowed to, he would play it twenty-four hours a day.

Parker, one year younger than Ty, doesn't possess his brother's athletic abilities, but his determination to succeed and to not be outdone by anyone makes him a worthy opponent. He possesses a photographic memory that proves to be an asset when his sister gets them involved in one of her many schemes.

After meeting the Old One, the kids have the ability to communicate through their Inuas, a gift that is only bestowed upon shamans. An Inua is the spiritual occupant (spirit helper) that resides in all living and inanimate things.

The Old One opens up a world to the kids they never knew existed, but when they discover at the dig site the first amulet made by the first shaman, they learn they are protected in a manner mortal man has only been able to dream about. The amulet gives them protection from anything that would harm them and even allows them to approach and travel with dangerous animals. It also allows them to encounter the legendary Inuit "Little People."

Chapter 1

The Footprint

Thursday, December 12, 1985

Dear Diary,

    When Dad and Mr. Duncan spoke of finding what they thought was a small footprint at the dig site, I never dreamed it would lead to such an adventure. Until then, I didn't even know the Little People existed!

    Amy

Max Trapps and his assistant Bill Duncan arrived at the dig and commenced their daily duties. They were falling into a familiar routine as the work progressed.

    "Do you think we'll ever find out why this settlement was built so far from any shoreline?" Bill asked.

"I don't know," replied Max. "You can tell from the terrain no river has ever flowed past this point, and we're a long ways from the Hudson Bay. I'll bet if we could converse with the old shaman, Kadluk, he would be able to shed some light on the subject."

"You're probably right. If anybody could shed some light, it would be him." Bill walked to the site he had been excavating the day before. He looked at the ground and couldn't believe his eyes.

"Come here, Max. What do you make of this? Is that a footprint I'm looking at or am I seeing things?"

Max walked up to Bill and looked where he was pointing. "You're right. It does look like a little footprint," he remarked, staring at the tiny lone print that was about two and a half centimeters long in the dirt.

"Now who or what do you think made that impression?" asked Bill.

"I'll tell you what it could be, seeing as there's only one. That's about the size of Amys' doll's foot. If she had her doll out here, that would explain it, although I can't see her bringing it out. It usually doesn't stray far from her dresser," Max replied.

"You're probably right. It looks like it was

14

made by a doll's foot or a kamik. If it had been a shoe, there would be a defined outline from the sole and heel. Is it a special doll?" Bill asked.

"Yes, it's her Cabbage Patch doll. Her Aunt Judy gave it to her at Christmas, and she named it Sir Colbert Frederick. She adopted it and everything; she's even got papers." Max chuckled as he recalled the events that had taken place during the adoption process.

"Who knows what made that impression? It could have been anything. If there were more than one, we might have a real mystery on our hands, but it's probably nothing. No one I know could make a footprint that small." Bill brushed off the encounter with a laugh, and the little indentation in the ground was forgotten as the excavation commenced in earnest.

Neither of the men saw David, the little person, observing them from the safety of the packing crates at the far end of the tent. As David watched the two men, he wondered if these were two of the three kabloonas he had heard the spirits talking about. Could they be the ones the Old One had befriended and was showing the ways of the shaman? If they were, where was the third one? The spirits had said there were three, and one was a girl. Where was the girl?

David tried to talk to the two men's Inuas. *"By what name are you known?"* he asked, but they would not respond. He tried again. *"Are you the kabloonas the Old One is training to be shamans?"*

Again his question was greeted by silence. David had only encountered one kabloona many years ago, and he hadn't had much to do with him. Kabloonas, he knew, didn't live by the old ways; they brought new tools and lived by customs that were strange and confusing.

David didn't know what to do. Should he leave this place and try to find the Old One, or should he wait here and see if the Old One's students showed up?

He needed to decide soon, because time was of the essence. The spirits had talked about the extraordinary abilities of the students, and David was sure they could help him. Staying here, he decided, was his best course of action. If the students were indeed here, the Old One wouldn't be far away. He would be close by in case the students needed help. Yes, he would wait, David decided.

*   *   *

The evening meal found everyone together in the kitchen.

"Did you ask Amy about Sir Colbert Frederick?" Bill asked Max.

"No, I didn't," her father replied.

"What about my doll?" Amy asked.

"What Bill is referring to is a small indentation we found in the dirt this morning at the dig. It was about the same size as your doll's foot. I thought maybe you had taken your doll to the dig," Max replied.

"I haven't taken it to the dig," Amy stated.

"No, old Sir Colbert doesn't leave her room; she's afraid he'll get dirty," Ty laughed.

"If it wasn't the doll, what could it be?" Bill asked.

"I doubt we'll ever know," Max replied.

"Ishigaq," Mr. Munro said.

"What?" Everyone spoke in unison as they turned to look at the mine superintendent.

"Ishigaq, the Little People," Mr. Munro explained.

"Whew," Mrs. Munro said. "For a minute I thought you had something stuck in your throat and that you were choking."

"What little people?" Max asked.

"The Inuit say little people live along the

17

coast," Mr. Munro replied. "They call them Ishigaq, which means Little People."

"Have you seen any little people, Mr. Munro?" Amy asked.

"No, dear, that's all I know about them. I haven't met anyone who has ever seen one," Mr. Munro replied.

"Do you believe there are little people living along the shoreline?" Nadine asked.

"I don't know…So many things have happened here that I didn't believe were possible that I just don't know what to believe anymore," Mr. Munro replied.

"Well, we're a long ways from the shoreline of Hudson Bay. If it was an Ishigaq, what would he be doing so far inland?" Mrs. Munro asked with a smile on her face.

"I didn't say it was an Ishigaq; I just mentioned it as a possible cause of the impression," her husband clarified.

"There are a number of Eastern cultures that believe little people inhabit their shorelines," Max told the group.

As his children looked at him with excitement, their mother added, "But no one has ever seen one to substantiate the claim."

"That's right; no one that we know of," Max said.

As the adults continued to argue the pros and cons of the existence of little people, Amy talked to her brothers through her Inua.

"Well, what do you think? Are the Ishigaq real or not?" she asked.

"It's true, Amy. The Inuit believe the Little People live along the coast, just as they do. They are about a foot tall and they wear caribou clothing," Parker informed his siblings.

"I suppose you learned that at the library?" Ty asked.

"Of course I did. They are also believed to be protective of the Inuit and will come to their aid when attacked. When aroused, the Little People can grow to the size of a full-grown Inuk, and they are fierce fighters. But it is said that they are very shy and are seldom seen," Parker advised.

"Leave it to you to know all that!" Amy replied.

The kids' attention snapped back to the adults when Mr. Munro asked a question.

"Would anyone like to take a trip to Rankin Inlet with me tomorrow?" he asked.

All thoughts of the Ishigaq faded into the past at the thought of the new adventure awaiting them, and Mr. Munro didn't need to wait for an answer. He knew what it would be, and his van would be full of excited passengers.

chapter ii

A Trip to Rankin Inlet

The morning brought fresh vigor to the group, and they were soon in the van and heading for Rankin.

Everyone was happy, and the children spontaneously burst into song.

"Ninety-nine bottles of cheer on the wall, ninety-nine bottles of cheer, if one of those bottles should happen to fall, ninety-eight bottles of cheer on the wall."

On they sang as the van bounced over the snow-covered rocky road westward towards the ice bridge some fifteen kilometers away. The ice bridge would provide access to the south shore of the

Meliadine River for the final leg of their journey into Rankin. It was still dark, and would be for another couple of hours.

"I can see the lights of Rankin!" Amy suddenly cried.

Looking ahead, the group could make out the settlement lights illuminating the dark sky as if a beacon were calling them to come and visit. They still had ten minutes of travel before they reached their destination, and they watched as the light grew brighter.

"It's like finding an oasis in the middle of the desert," Amy remarked.

"You've got that right. There's nothing out here but the mine and Rankin. We might as well be in the desert," Ty commented.

"What are we going to do in town?" Parker asked.

"What do you want to do?" his father asked him.

"I don't know," Parker replied.

"I have a meeting to attend at the government office. Max, you and Bill can come with me if you like. We can drop the women and kids at the co-op and they can look around there and then go to the Hudson Bay Store. We can all meet at the hotel restaurant for lunch and then head for home," Mr. Munro offered.

"Sounds like a good plan to me," Max replied, and everyone nodded in agreement.

"I want to look at the ivory carvings and see what's for sale," Amy told everyone.

"While you're doing that, I'll look at the wall hangings and see if there are any new ones. Some of the finest hangings you will ever encounter come from Rankin," Mrs. Munro informed the group.

"I want to see them also," added Nadine.

"Well, I want to see if they have any new hockey sticks. The two I brought with me are getting pretty busted up. I don't know how much longer the tape is going to hold them together," Ty remarked.

"Maybe if you weren't practicing your slap shot all the time, they would last longer," Amy told Ty.

Ty ignored Amy's advice.

"Yeah, it's time I looked for a new stick too. And maybe they've got the new Spiderman comic. I want to get it if it's out," Parker added.

After shopping at the co-op and the Bay, the little group headed for the restaurant and the rendezvous with the men. Just before entering the hotel restaurant, they heard a man's voice singing.

"She lost her shoe, she lost her shoe, she lost her shoe, I saaaaay,

She lost her shoe, she lost her shoe, down by the baaaaay."

The singing man crossed the street and disappeared.

"Who was that? He sure has a strange accent," Amy commented.

"I have no idea, but he doesn't sound like he's from around here," Mrs. Munro replied.

"Why worry about him? We'll probably never see him again," Ty remarked as they entered the restaurant.

"You're right. He just seems odd, and he's dressed funny," Amy said.

The strange man was soon forgotten as the group was seated and began to hungrily peruse the lunch menu.

chapter iii

all is not as it seems

They were just finishing lunch when Constable Charlie entered the restaurant.

"Hello everyone; what brings you to town today? I saw your van outside and wondered who was visiting," he said as he pulled up a chair and ordered a coffee.

"I had a meeting with the government boys, and everyone else came along for the ride," Mr. Munro replied.

"I see you have all your children and none are missing," Constable Charlie stated.

"Why, is there a problem?" Nadine asked.

"I don't think so, but then again, I really don't know. You haven't had any new families arrive at the mine with kids I don't know about, have you?" the constable asked.

"No, these are the only kids staying at the mine. We haven't had any new arrivals since your last visit. Which I might add has been a while, which I expect you will be correcting quite soon. Am I right?" Mr. Munro asked

"What's wrong? Why are you asking about kids? Is there something we should know?" Nadine asked. This talk about missing kids was starting to concern her.

"There's a rumor going around that some kids are missing. I've checked every family in Rankin, Chesterfield Inlet, and Whale Cove, and I also had the neighboring detachments check their families. We can't find anyone missing; everyone seems to be accounted for. I don't know if it was someone overhearing a conversation and drawing a conclusion or what, but it's really created a lot of leg work, checking up on everyone. All the families know where their kids are, but some have told me they've heard some kids are missing. It's just that no one knows whose kids they are or where they're from or how this all started. I've been looking for Kadluk; he may be able to shed some light on this subject, but I haven't been able to find him. I don't know if he's in the settlement or not because no one has seen him," Constable Charlie said.

"What would he have to do with kids?" Nadine asked.

"I'll tell you about something that happened last spring and then you can tell me if you think he would have any knowledge about this. Mary Tagak and her little brother Johnny who was just a toddler at the time were playing on the ice in the bay. The wind came up and the fast ice broke away and got blown into the bay. Mary was able to jump to shore but little Johnny was swept away. It was about a half hour later when Mary told me what had happened, and I went to see Mary's mother. By now the wind was really up and it was almost blizzard conditions with the wind picking the snow off the ground. I told her with the conditions the way they were, there wasn't much we could do until the weather broke.

"Mary's mother said to me, 'Does the Old One know?' Usually when he's in the settlement you see him around, but I hadn't seen him for a few days. I told her I didn't know if he knew or not and I really didn't think any more about it. When I got back to the office, I called Yellowknife and arranged for our twin Otter to come over to do a search. The pilots were to fly to Baker Lake and then come over the next morning after the weather broke. I contacted some fellows to be spotters when the plane arrived. Under the circumstances, there wasn't anything else I could do.

"The next morning the weather was clearing and the wind had died down. I got everybody ready to go and went to tell Mary's mother what we were doing. When I arrived at their house, she met me at the door and said everything was okay and that Johnny was sleeping in his bed.

"I didn't believe her, so I went to the bedroom and checked, and sure enough the little fellow was in bed sleeping. Now you tell me how that toddler got off that ice floe and into his bed. He was just learning how to walk. It was near blizzard conditions and he was adrift on pack ice in the bay. I asked Mary's mother how he got home and she said she didn't know, he was in his bed when she got up.

I was baffled, but there was nothing else to do but call off the search. Then I remembered she had asked me if the Old One knew about the incident. I asked her about it and what she meant. She said she didn't mean anything by it; she just wanted to know if the Old One knew because he always looks out for the children. I saw Kadluk a few days later, and through an interpreter I asked him about the incident. All he would say was that what is supposed to happen will happen.

I just can't figure him out," Constable Charlie concluded. "I don't know if he was involved or not, and I guess I'll never know unless he wants me to know."

Everyone sat in muted silence, pondering this event.

Silently, Amy talked to her brothers through her Inua.

"I'll bet the Old One saved the little guy," she said

"It sounds just like something he would do," Ty remarked.

"Yep that would be the Old One. Do something and don't take credit for it or even acknowledge that you had a hand in it," Parker added.

"That's quite a story," Nadine remarked.

"Does this happen often?" Amy asked Constable Charlie out loud.

"Does what happen often?" he replied.

"Rumors, or people overhearing other people's conversations, starting investigations?" Amy asked.

"It sure does," replied Constable Charlie.

The kids really liked Constable Charlie. He always took the time to explain things to them and he didn't treat them like little kids. He went out of his way to talk to them and make them feel at home.

"Don't forget, the coffee at the mine is just as good as the coffee here, and you're welcome to as much as you want anytime," Mr. Munro told Constable Charlie, shaking his hand as the man prepared to depart.

*   *   *

Leaving the restaurant, the group heard him before they saw him.

"Hey! There he is again," Ty remarked.

"She lost her shoe, she lost her shoe, she lost her shoe, I saaaaay.

She lost her shoe, she lost her shoe, down by the baaaaay."

The singing faded as the man with the noticeable limp walked away from them, rounded a corner, and disappeared from sight.

"Who was that?" Amy asked. "He sure seems happy."

31

"Yes, he does. I wonder what he's been up to? I don't know much about that guy, but I've never seen him so jovial before. I've seen him in the other settlements, and each settlement seems to know him by a different name. Here he's known as Peg-Leg-Pete. Over in Coral Harbor he's known as Pirate Bill. Up in Repulse Bay, he's South-Seas-Sam. So I guess you know as much about him as I do," Mr. Munro said.

"Where did he get that funny hat?" Parker asked.

"Well, believe it or not, he had an Inuk lady make if for him. It seems he fancies himself as a pirate, so he had her make him a pirate hat out of sealskin," Mr. Munro replied.

"Does he really have a peg leg?" Ty queried.

"I don't know. Someone told me he lost his leg to a great white shark years ago when he was pirating in the Caribbean. When he's in Rankin, he limps, but when I saw him in Coral Harbor and Repulse Bay, he wasn't limping."

"Where did he come from?" Amy asked.

"Some say he came up from the Caribbean on a summer re-supply ship. People have told me he's a pirate, a descendent of the famous pirate Captain

Kidd of the seventeenth century, but he's never inquired about a job with us, so I really don't know for sure," Mr. Munro replied.

"Jiminy-Willie-Peppers, a real live pirate!" Parker howled.

"Yes, he may very well be, and then again he could just be one of the strange characters that are attracted to the North for one reason or another," Mr. Munro commented as the group climbed into the van.

"It seems weird. I wonder if we'll ever see him again," Ty said as they drove out of Rankin.

"Where were we in the song, before we stopped?" asked Amy.

"Parker, you should know," Nadine said.

"I wasn't singing, Mom, and I really wasn't paying attention. I was thinking about something else," Parker replied.

"Okay, from the top," Amy said, and they burst into song.

"Ninety-nine bottles of cheer on the wall, ninety-nine bottles of cheer…"

When there are only four hours of daylight, the day passes quickly. Sure enough, darkness had set in when the group arrived back at the mine.

33

who are you

The morning after the trip to Rankin found the kids alone at the dig. Max and Bill would be coming out later after their conference call to Yellowknife. Amy as usual was getting the equipment ready for the day's work while Ty and Parker were checking out the equipment to see if anything new had been added to the inventory that could be utilized in one of their many imaginary games.

"Come on you two and give me a hand; Dad and Bill will be here before long and I want this equipment ready," Amy called to the boys.

"We'll be right there," Ty replied.

"Well, I'm not doing anything else until you get here," Amy said and sat down. As she looked toward her brothers, she noticed a little person walking towards them.

"Whose child is that?" she asked, pointing towards the little person.

"That's not a child; that's a full grown man. Look how small he is!" exclaimed Ty.

"Jiminy-Willie-Peppers, I've never seen anyone that small!" cried Parker.

"Look, he's dressed in Caribou clothing, the traditional dress of the People, just like the Old One," Amy squealed.

"Where did he come from?" Ty wanted to know.

"Who are you?" Amy asked through her Inua.

"How come you're so small?" Ty asked.

"How come you're so big?" David, the little person, replied.

"Ty, don't be rude!" Amy scolded her brother.

"I'm not being rude; I just asked a question," Ty replied.

"It's okay; I'm sure Ty is just curious," said the little person. *"It doesn't hurt to ask questions. And you were probably wondering the same thing. I doubt you've seen many people my size. I'm David of the Little People. You must be the Old One's friends, the ones he's training to be shamans. Otherwise we wouldn't be able to communicate through our Inuas,"* the little person replied.

36

"Yes, we are the Old One's friends. You must also be a shaman or we wouldn't be able to talk to each other," Amy replied, looking at the small man before her.

"How come the Old One told you about us?" Parker asked.

"He didn't. I've heard the spirits sing your praises. They tell me you will help the People in their time of need; is this not so?" David looked intently at each of the kids.

"Yes, we will help anyone we can when they're in trouble, if we can," Amy replied.

"Then I've come to the right place. My journey has been long and not without peril," David informed the kids.

"How can we help?" Amy inquired.

"Be careful, Amy; you don't know what you're getting into," cautioned Ty.

"He hasn't told us anything yet, Ty," Amy shot back.

"I'll bet it's going to be a good adventure," Parker enthusiastically offered.

"Amayersuk, the old lady who steals misbehaving children, has taken all the children from our village and we don't know where they are. The women are sad without their children to look after and teach. The mood

in the village is utter despair," David sadly explained to the kids.

"*Why would she steal the children? I thought she was supposed to return the children when they repented,"* Parker inquired.

"*No one knows why she is doing this, but she must have them. I have checked everywhere and they cannot be found. I've prayed to the deities and asked for their help. The villagers have confessed their sins and asked for guidance and nothing seems to work. I've sent my spirit helpers to ask questions and no one answers. I travelled the road of sorrows to find Sedna for help. Sedna told me to start a quest and the path to Amayersuk's house would be revealed to me. My assistant is preparing the mask I must use during the ceremony to start the quest,"* David informed the group.

"*Then you don't know for sure if Amayersuk has the children,"* Amy stated.

"*They are nowhere to be found, so she must have them. It is said that once Amayersuk has them, she will try to encourage them to be naughty. Then she will be able to keep them longer. If they repent and show proper respect, Amayersuk will have to return them to their families. She is not allowed to interfere with anyone who behaves. Bad manners is one of the traits she thrives on. Kindness and obedience, she cannot accept. But something must be wrong; she is doing something she should not be doing,"* David told the kids.

"The road of sorrows…When we went to see Sedna, we travelled the road of shadows," Parker said.

"Every quest is different; the quest you take will determine which road you must travel," David told Parker.

"This doesn't sound very good," Ty remarked, looking searchingly at Amy.

"Where would she take the children?" Amy questioned David.

"I don't know, but I have heard that she takes them to Lands End," David replied.

"Lands End? I've never heard of it. Where is it?" Amy asked.

"Many days journey to the north. I've heard there are many hardships to endure. No one has ever returned from Lands End that I know of," David replied.

"Why do you think we can help if no one has ever returned from there? It sounds like a one way ticket to me!" Ty stated rather excitedly.

"Ty, don't go making assumptions without knowing the facts," Amy scolded her brother.

"Without knowing the facts?" Ty shouted. *"The fact that no one has ever returned from there should be reason enough for not trying to go there. What do you think Parker?"* Ty looked at his brother for support.

"You're stating a pretty strong position for not

going. I haven't heard any reasons so far that would make me think we'd have any chance of returning when no one else has ever done it," Parker stated.

"Oh, how bad can it be? We've got to help this gentleman if we can. After all, he did travel a long way to recruit us," Amy stated.

"I don't know…I think we should ask the Old One," Ty replied.

"That's a good idea. The Old One is just the person to ask. If anyone can make the trip, he can," Amy said.

"How do you propose we ask him? We don't even know where he is," Ty remarked.

"Listen," Parker said.

"Listen to what? I don't hear anything," Ty replied.

"I thought I heard dogs," Parker said.

"It is dogs. I can hear them. That means the Old One is coming!" Amy ran towards the tent door.

The door to the huge tent swung open and there stood the Old One with the wind whipping the snow in a circular motion around him.

"Boy, are we glad to see you!" Amy said, still talking through her Inua.

"Where did you come from?" Ty asked.

"It matters not. Why are the Little People's kids missing?" the Old One asked.

"We don't know, but David of the Little People thinks Amayersuk has taken them because they were being naughty and not listening to their mothers," Amy explained.

"I see," said the Old One.

"How did you know the kids are missing? Ty asked.

"The Raven told me," the Old One replied.

"Why would the Raven tell you about the kids?" Ty asked again.

"This morning when the Raven let me use his eyes, he told me that David of the Little People had used his eyes to search the pack ice in search of the missing kids. He said David told him the kids had been playing on the fast ice when they had been told not to. The ice broke free and drifted into the bay. The women didn't notice this until the ice was far out into the bay and the kids were nowhere to be found. After David searched the ice through the Raven's eyes, he determined that Amayersuk had taken the kids because they were being naughty by disobeying their parents. The Raven told me David was going to come to the ancient village site to seek your assistance because he knew this was where he would find you. David is here, is he not?" the Old One asked.

"Boy, that's the longest explanation I've ever heard the Old One give. Usually he disregards the

41

question or gives the briefest of explanations," Parker said privately to Ty.

"Yes, he is here, sitting with the boys," Amy replied.

David had been standing on the opposite side of Ty, hidden from the Old One's view.

"We do not have any time to waste. We leave immediately," the Old One said as he spun on his heel and returned to his dog team.

"Why do we have to leave right now?" Amy called after him.

"We have to go to David's village so that he can complete his ritual that will show us the path we must take to find Amayersuk," the Old One replied.

"Oh!" Amy said, and she and David and the boys hurried after the Old One.

*   *   *

With David and the kids loaded on the komatik, the group was soon flying over the tundra on its way towards the shore and David's village.

David stood at the front of the komatik, holding onto the leather lashings to steady himself, pointing the way for Kadluk.

"Doesn't he remind you of a chariot driver, the way he's holding onto the lashings? It looks like he's driving the komatik," Amy said to Ty and Parker through her Inua. It was much easier than trying to talk out loud while speeding over the snow.

"Yes, he does," the boys replied.

"How far do we have to go?" Amy asked.

"It's not far. You will see it as soon as we reach the shoreline," David advised her.

"I always enjoy the komatik rides. They're a little rough, but the Old One sure doesn't waste time travelling," Parker remarked.

"Yeah, but sometimes it kind of jars your teeth," Ty added.

"Look ahead. I can see David's village! Boy, are those houses ever small. If I wasn't looking for the village, I would have missed it completely. Old One, their houses are built just like the People's houses. Why are all your igloos built like domes?" Amy asked.

"I know," Parker answered before Kadluk could speak. *"It's because that's the strongest structure man can build. The dome shape can withstand even the strongest winds."*

"What do you mean?" Amy asked.

43

"*The wind bends and flows around it when the wind meets the dome and doesn't harm it,*" Parker replied.

"*Is that right, Old One?*" Ty asked.

"*He is correct,*" Kadluk said.

"*Yep, all the ancient civilizations used the dome. Farmers today still use it,*" Parker informed the group.

"*What do you mean?*" Amy asked.

"*Remember when we were on our cousin's farm last year at harvest? Remember they didn't have enough bins to hold all the grain they harvested? Remember how Uncle Newt piled it in the open field? Using his auger, he piled it into a dome-shaped structure. That way, the wind just blew around it and didn't blow the kernels of grain away,*" Parker explained.

"*Leave it to you to remember something like that,*" Amy replied.

"*Hey! We've been to this area before. How come we've never seen his village?*" Parker asked.

"*You're right, Parker; we've been here lots of times,*" Ty added.

"*If the Little People don't want you to see their village, you won't be able to see it. They're very shy and secretive. It they don't want you in their world, they won't let you in,*" Kadluk advised the kids.

"*Then this is an honour, being asked to help them and being able to visit their village?*" Amy asked.

44

"It is indeed a privilege to visit their village and a great honour to be asked to help them in their time of sorrow. Very few ever get to see, let alone meet, the Little People."

"I think they're cute. They're so small; their children must be just tiny," Amy remarked.

"Hey, who is that and what is he doing?" Ty asked, pointing to a Little Person who appeared to be whittling away at a piece of wood as big as himself.

The villagers were sitting in a semi-circle in front of this person, and although they were sad and crying, they watched him intently. Between this Inuk and the villagers, a small fire burned. The villagers were ready and awaiting the arrival of the shamans.

"That's my assistant; he's finishing the mask I will need for the ceremony," David advised the group.

"It's only a face mask," Parker observed.

"It's a full body mask!" David replied.

"Oh, yeah. For you, I guess it would be a full body mask. Why are you making it so big?" Parker asked.

"My vision revealed to me how the mask was to be made. It has to be a full body mask to represent the heavy burden placed on me to complete my quest to return the children to my village. The mouth of the mask is sad, depicting the sadness of the Little People because their

45

children have been taken. See the hands folded across the chest with the fingers tightly clenched? This represents how Amayersuk has taken and holds the children against their will. Her rigidity is denying the Little People the pleasure of the company of their children. The black line across the nose from cheek to cheek separates the sadness from the joy. The eyes are happy and full of joy. Eight little bone projections protrude from the head, each with a small carving of a child attached. The carvings are attached to the bone by strips of leather made from caribou hide. The carvings hang free, displaying the freedom the children will enjoy when they are returned to their village," David informed the group.

It was apparent the assistant had taken great care to carve the mask exactly as David had envisioned it. Beside the assistant lay a drum, which he picked up and started to beat as David moved behind the mask.

Taking the mask in both hands, David began to chant the secret chants of the shaman.

Boom-boom-boom went the drum as the assistant beat a steady cadence.

"Aiiieee," chanted David.

Kadluk and the kids joined David and chanted the secret chants of the shaman, asking their tutelary spirits, their guardian spirits, to protect them and assist them during their journey to

46

retrieve the children. They called on their ancestors' spirits to stand by them and lend them their strength in their time of need during their long journey. They called upon the villagers to lend them their Inyusuq, the powerful forces that reside in all individuals and serve as the source of good health, stamina, willpower, and energy.

Boom-boom-boom went the drum, and a trance like state overtook the group.

The villagers called on the shamans to be brave and strong, and they offered their Inyusuq to be used on the arduous journey they were about to undertake.

David jumped out from behind the mask and declared, *"The way has been shown to me. I have seen the trail we must follow to find Amayersuk. The mask, Old One, destroy the mask."*

Kadluk picked up the mask and flung it into the fire, where it was immediately consumed by flames.

"Why did you want the mask destroyed?" Amy asked.

"The mask was vacant after our ceremony, and I didn't want a Tarrak to inhabit it," David replied.

"What do we do now?" Amy asked.

"Now our journey begins," David replied.

Chapter V

i see the way

"*Quick everyone; get on the komatik. My dog team awaits,*" Kadluk said.

The kids were soon on the komatik, with David again standing at the front holding onto the leather lashings.

"*David, what path did your vision tell you to take?*" Amy asked.

"*Straight west until we hit the big lake, then we travel straight north from there,*" David replied.

"*Point the way, David,*" Kadluk called out.

With a crack of Kadluk's whip, the dog team was up and running westward. The miles rapidly fell by the wayside as the group followed David's directions.

"*I can see the lake up ahead,*" Parker called out.

"*Yes, I can see it. We will soon be turning north,*" replied David.

49

When they reached the lakeshore, Kadluk turned the dogs north and on they sped.

"Old One, what are those things up ahead?" Amy asked.

"I don't know. They look like Inukshuks but they are awfully big," replied Kadluk.

"You don't know! Do you mean we've finally found something you know nothing about?" Ty asked.

"Ty don't be rude," Amy scolded.

"I'm not being rude! I just can't believe we've found something the Old One has never seen," Ty replied.

As the group drew nearer, they could see the Inukshuks more clearly and they were indeed very tall, standing just over twenty feet high.

"David, exactly what did your vision reveal to you?" Kadluk asked.

"My vision told me to travel straight west to the big lake and then straight north. It said not to deviate from this path," David replied.

"Old One, you must have traveled this area before. Why don't you know about these Inukshuks? They would be very hard to miss; they can be seen for miles in all directions," Amy said.

"I'll bet it has to do with the vision. If we hadn't traveled the precise route the vision revealed to us, we wouldn't have seen them either," Parker declared.

50

"*You may be right, Parker. The location of these Inukshuks may only be known by Amayersuk, and perhaps traveling an exact trail is the only way to find them and her,*" Kadluk said.

"*Look at them. They are exactly the same in every detail,*" Amy remarked.

"*You're right, Amy. They are identical,*" Ty said.

"*Old One, don't you know where Amayersuk lives?*" Parker asked.

"*No, I don't. I have never had any reason to find her before. Until now, she has never abused her authority,*" Kadluk responded.

"*Then you don't know if this is the right trail to Amayersuk's or not?*" Amy asked.

"*No, I don't know. We'll ask the Inukshuks. Maybe they can tell us if this is the right trail,*" Kadluk replied.

"*Oh, great. We don't even know if this is the right path. We could be lost,*" Ty stated.

"*If we keep following this trail, we will be passing directly between the two Inukshuks,*" Parker advised the group.

"*You're right, Parker. We are heading directly between them,*" Amy replied.

Kadluk stopped the dog team between the two Inukshuks. "*Who built you?*" he asked.

There was no reply.

51

Again he asked, *"Who built you?"*

The silence was deafening.

"Why won't they answer you?" Amy asked.

"I don't know," Kadluk replied. *"Why won't you answer my questions?"* he asked the Inukshuks.

"The giant woman who built us doesn't want us to talk to anyone," one of the Inukshuks replied.

"Do you know what the giant woman's name is?" Kadluk asked.

"She never told us what her name is, but when she passes by with the children, they are always crying and pleading with her and saying, 'Please, Amayersuk, take us home; we promise to be good.' She is always happiest when the kids are naughty and she's not happy at all when she has to return them," the Inukshuk advised.

"Why doesn't she want you to talk to anyone?" Kadluk asked.

"I don't know. She never said," replied the Inukshuk.

"Why are you talking to us if you were told not to?" Kadluk continued.

"The only people who pass this way are always with Amayersuk, so we were curious as to why you are here without her," the Inukshuk replied.

"The children of the Little People are missing and we believe that she has them. We are on a quest to return

the children to their village. Did you see Amayersuk with the children?" Kadluk asked.

"Yes, she went north with them but she hasn't come back yet, so they are still with her," the Inukshuk replied.

"How do you know they are still with her?" Kadluk asked.

"When she goes north, the kids are with her, and when she returns from the north and heads south, she takes the kids back to their villages and then they are no longer with her," the Inukshuk explained.

"Does anyone else ever use this trail?" Kadluk asked.

"Sometimes there is a man with Amayersuk and the kids, but not very often," said the Inukshuk.

"What is his name?" Kadluk asked.

"I don't know, but I've heard Amayersuk call him Boogey or something like that," the Inukshuk reply.

"Boogey! That name means nothing to me," Kadluk remarked.

"Maybe it means boogie-woogie, like the dance," laughed Parker.

"I don't think so," Ty remarked.

"Be serious, you two. Where does this trail lead?" Amy asked the Inukshuk.

"I don't know," the Inukshuk replied.

"What do you mean, you don't know? You stand

guard at the trail, don't you?" Ty inquired.

"No one has ever returned who could tell us," came the reply.

"We're in deep trouble!" Ty howled.

"Ty, you may be right." Parker looked worried.

"Quiet, you two! Does this land lead to Lands End?" Amy wanted to know.

"I don't know," replied the Inukshuk

"Why does Amayersuk use this trail?" Ty asked.

"I don't know; she doesn't talk to me. She's always too busy to talk," came the reply.

Amy asked, *"Busy doing what?"*

The Inukshuk replied, *"She's busy looking after the children who are with her."*

"Does she always have kids with her?" Kadluk asked.

"No, not always. Sometimes she's alone," came the reply.

"Enough!" Kadluk cried. *"David, point the way. We must continue our journey."*

His whip cracked, and the dogs once again strained at their leads as the komatik literally flew over the frozen ground.

Chapter vi

The Encounter

The miles flew by as the group continued north in search of Amayersuk and the children.

The mood changed as soon as they started their descent into the valley. The air was filled with apprehension; all their senses were alert and they were ready to react to the slightest provocation. Danger was nearby; they could feel it but could not see it. Was it a threat not of their world? Could their amulet protect them? Only time and many miles of travel would answer these anxious questions.

The group continued, not knowing what fate lay ahead. Finally, far ahead at the base of the mountains, they saw a faint glow. They heard the cackling voice of the giant woman, Amayersuk, before they saw her.

"Listen, there's another voice. It sounds like a man's voice," Amy said.

Sure enough, the hearty laugh of a man split the silence of the land while Amayersuk joined the laughter with her cackling. In the background, the group could hear the voices of the children crying and pleading with their tormentors.

"*Old One, who is the man with Amayersuk?*" Amy cried.

"*I don't know. I don't know who would be with her,*" Kadluk replied as he gazed ahead, trying to make out who could be with Amayersuk.

"*It looks like Peg-Leg-Pete. He's wearing his pirate hat!*" Parker yelled.

"*You're right! It is him! I wonder what he's doing here?*" Amy said.

*　　　*　　　*

"*Amayersuk, who is that?*" Peg-Leg-Pete pointed at the group warily approaching.

"*I don't know,*" Amayersuk replied.

"*I thought you said no one would dare enter your camp uninvited?*"

"*No one would dare!*" Amayersuk sternly declared.

Her laughter stopped, and only the crying of the captive children could be heard as Kadluk's group neared the village.

Amayersuk and Peg-Leg-Pete stood up, and Amayersuk was the first to speak.

"Who dares to approach my...?" She stopped in mid-sentence when she saw Kadluk. He reminded her of someone from a long time ago, but she couldn't quite remember whom. Suddenly, visions of a small boy came to her. She had tried to make the boy misbehave so she could take him from his family, but he wouldn't misbehave, so she'd left him alone and concentrated on the kids she could more easily persuade.

She recalled that the boy had always been with his grandfather, and if her memory served her correctly, the grandfather had been a shaman. What were their names? She tried to remember but couldn't. The boy, although very young, was not afraid of anything.

Could this possibly be the same young boy from so long ago? That young boy had been different from the other children, and that was why she'd left him alone.

Amayersuk had the same feeling now when she saw him, and it was a feeling she didn't like. No person had ever found her camp, let alone walked in

58

unannounced, yet here he was, standing in front of her. She shook her head, trying to scrape the cobwebs from her mind. She felt it was important to recall the name of that boy, but no matter how hard she tried, it failed to come to her.

It mattered not, she finally decided. No one had ever stood up to her, and she quickly dismissed any thought of the boy.

"I am Kadluk. We have come for the children," the shaman replied.

"Look, there are the children. She has them in some kind of pen. Look how small they are," said Parker.

"The adults we met in the village were small, but the kids are really small," cried Amy.

"I'll say they're small. The biggest one can't be more than six inches tall, and the smallest one is only about four inches," remarked Ty.

"They look okay. They don't seem to be hurt. Why are they crying?" Parker asked.

"They probably miss their families and want to go home," Amy explained.

"You have no authority here. Be gone before you feel my wrath!" shrieked Amayersuk.

"You have no authority to hold the children. They have atoned for their transgressions and must be returned to their parents who are grieving their disappearance," Kadluk firmly stated.

"Who questions my authority? I will say when the kids are to be returned," cackled Amayersuk in her high-pitched voice. *"Be gone with you before I unleash my fury!"*

In spite of her threatening words, Amayersuk stared at Kadluk in disbelief. How was it that he showed no fear? She had stared down shamans before, but this one was different. A sickening feeling gripped her as she stared at the man before her. She had never before feared any shaman, but something about this one told her he was not to be trifled with.

With an unsteady voice, Amayersuk tried to save face. She had met her match and she knew it. *"I will take the children home tonight,"* she said, trying to muster as much authority as she could.

"You will take the kids home now, where they belong. They have suffered enough, and so have their families, because of your folly!" Kadluk admonished her.

Amayersuk recoiled. No one had ever spoken to her in such a voice. She was getting confused, her confidence wavering. *"I...I said I will take them home tonight,"* she repeated rather weakly.

"I said you will take them home now, and in the future you will not abuse your authority again," Kadluk firmly stated.

As Kadluk stood before Amayersuk, she trembled. What was it about this shaman that gave him this air of authority? Who was he? She needed to know. He was no ordinary shaman. His very presence demanded respect. He scared Amayersuk, and she had never been scared before. Indeed, the very mention of her name struck terror in the hearts of those who heard it.

Every Inuk could tell a tale of horror relating to Amayersuk. She touched everyone's life at one time or another as the People journeyed through life. None of the experiences were good, and they left everyone trembling with terror. Some said she was a cannibal. Some said she had a big hole in her humped back where she kept the children.

"Are you known by another name?" Amayersuk meekly inquired. It was important that she avoid the wrath of this shaman should she ever encounter him again, but the name Kadluk was unknown to her.

"As I said before, I am Kadluk the shaman, but some know me as the Old One," Kadluk replied.

At that, Amayersuk felt her knees go weak, and she flinched. She would have fallen to the ground had not Peg-Leg-Pete standing beside her grabbed her arm and steadied her. She had never encountered the Old One before, but she had heard enough about him to know you didn't cross him if

61

you wanted to stay healthy. He was bigger than any legend who'd ever trod the earth before.

"What's the matter?" Peg-Leg-Pete demanded.

"It's…It's…It's him!" stammered Amayersuk, her mouth hanging open as she stared in disbelief. She cowered and tried to slink away.

"Who is it?" Peg-Leg-Pete asked.

"It's the Old One!" Amayersuk cried.

"Well, get rid of him!" Peg-Leg-Pete ordered.

"You don't understand," Amayersuk wailed. *"You don't cross the Old One."*

"Then I'll get rid of him," Peg-Leg-Pete bragged, pulling himself up to his full height.

"No, no!" howled Amayersuk. *"Don't do anything to rile the Old One."*

"Why not?" asked Peg-Leg Pete. *"He's only a man."*

"He's not like any man you've ever met," wailed Amayersuk.

"I'm not afraid of any man," Peg-Leg-Pete stated.

"You'd better be afraid of this man," Amayersuk answered. *"He's the only man brave enough to walk into my camp uninvited. He's a living legend of the People!"*

While Kadluk stood by, listening, watching, and waiting, the tone of Amayersuks' voice made Peg-Leg-Pete pause and reconsider his actions.

"Maybe I was a bit hasty, drawing the conclusion that you should get rid of him," Peg-Leg-Pete finally said. He could see that Amayersuk was scared almost out of her wits. If she was afraid of this man they called the Old One, maybe he should find out more about him before making any rash decisions.

"What would he have to do with the kids?" Peg-Leg-Pete asked.

"I don't know, but he wouldn't be here if something isn't wrong. Look behind him. He has brought the young kabloonas with him. I have heard they too possess the traits of a shaman. He has taken them under his wing and is teaching them the ways of the shaman. Look there on the komatik. That's David, a shaman of the Little People. They've come for the kids," Amayersuk concluded.

"I don't understand. I thought you were afraid of nothing, and here you are quaking in your kamiks at the mere sight of this man," Peg-Leg-Pete cried.

"You don't understand! This man can do things no one else can do. No one has ever bested the Old One. His feats are legendary. Even Nanook the mighty polar bear gives the Old One a wide berth, and the bear is afraid of nothing in his domain. No one tells the Old One what to do. If you know what's good for you, you leave the Old One alone." Amayersuk cowered anew.

"Why do you keep the children?" Kadluk suddenly demanded.

"I didn't mean anything by it. I meant them no harm," whined Amayersuk.

"Who is this Peg-Leg-Pete, and why won't his Inua speak to me?" demanded Kadluk.

"He doesn't like to talk to people, because when they find out who he really is they instantly dislike him," Amayersuk said.

"Well, who is he?" Kadluk repeated.

"To some he is known as the Boogeyman," replied Amayersuk.

At that, Peg-Leg-Pete tried to beat a hasty retreat to avoid the wrath of Kadluk. He didn't know Kadluk, but if Amayersuk was afraid of him, he'd better be too. Never before had he seen Amayersuk show fear when confronting any individual, and he'd never liked facing adults. He preferred terrorizing children; they were much easier to handle.

"Boogeyman! I know of no such man. What is a boogeyman?" Kadluk demanded.

"He…He sometimes takes errant children like I do," Amayersuk reluctantly explained.

"I've never heard of him!" exclaimed Kadluk. He turned to Amayersuk, dismissing Peg-Leg-Pete as if he weren't worthy of attention. *"You will return*

the children to their village right now!"

"Yes, yes, as you wish," Amayersuk replied, completely cowed.

Before departing the camp with the kids, Amayersuk prudently took a good look at Amy, Ty, Parker, and David. She wanted to remember them for the future. If they were friends of the Old One, she had better steer clear of them, too. She didn't want anything more to do with the Old One or his friends.

"Jiminy-Willie-Peppers," shouted Parker, "Amy, you and Ty must remember Mom and Dad telling us how Grandpa and Grandma used to threaten them when they were young. They used to tell them if they weren't good, the Boogeyman would come and get them. Remember how they used to say they would stay awake as long as they could when they went to bed for fear they would be taken by the Boogeyman?"

"You're right, Parker. I do remember them telling us that," replied Amy.

"Do you think Peg-Leg-Pete is the Boogeyman who used to terrorize Mom and Dad?" Ty peered intently at the man known as Peg-Leg-Pete.

"I don't know, but it sure looks like it." Parker shook his head.

Amayersuk wasted no time hitching her dog team up, and before the kids realized what she was doing, she was departing the camp. Amayersuk wanted to be clear of the Old One and his friends as fast as she could, and she and Peg-Leg-Pete beat a hasty retreat. They had suffered enough humiliation for one day.

"Did you see what she did with the children?" Amy asked Ty and Parker.

"No. She loaded them and took off so fast, I didn't really see what she did," Ty responded.

"Neither did I. Boy, she can sure move fast for being so big," Parker added.

"Did she put the children on her komatik or in the hole in the hump on her back?" Amy asked.

"I don't know. It happened too fast," Ty replied.

"Beats me." Parker shrugged his shoulders.

"I suppose now we'll never know whether she carries the kids in her hump or not," Amy remarked, a bit disappointed.

chapter vii

the feast

Kadluk and his group left Amayersuk's camp as soon as she'd departed with the kids. The trip home found the group in a jovial mood. Their journey had not been in vain. With the return of the kids, the village would be in a festive mood and everyone would be rejoicing.

David joined the kids on the komatik, since he no longer needed to stand in the front and point the way, and Kadluk let his dogs run free. They knew their destination and would make short work of the miles they had to travel.

Although Kadluk's dog team was the fastest the kids had ever seen, they never did catch sight of Amayersuk and her team on the return leg of their journey.

"Old One, do you think we'll ever have to visit Amayersuk's camp again?" Amy asked through her Inua.

Before Kadluk could answer, Ty said, *"I'll bet she thinks twice before she ever pulls a stunt like that again, with the dressing down Kadluk gave her."*

"I don't know Amy. I hope not," was all Kadluk said.

As they neared the Little People's village, the laughter and singing could be heard from afar.

"It sounds like the village is having a feast," Amy remarked.

"I hope they've saved some food for us. I'm starved," Ty stated.

"Leave it to you to think of your stomach," Amy said.

"Well, I'm hungry too," Parker added.

"I'm sure there will be enough for everyone," Amy replied.

When the group entered the village, they were escorted to the honored seats in the feast circle and offered the choicest cuts of meat. The elated Little People couldn't thank the group enough for returning their children. Loud burps and much passing of gas could be heard, the signs of a tremendous feast being enjoyed by all.

When their appetites were sated, it was time

69

for storytelling. This was the first time the Little People had hosted the Old One in their village. The storytelling prowess of this living legend was itself legendary, and they awaited his version of the events that had taken place.

Kadluk didn't disappoint. What's more, he took great pains to reenact the crucial role that David, the Little People's shaman, had played in the successful outcome of their journey. The people were amazed and sat in stunned silence as he replayed the events. David's stature grew in the eyes of his people and he was proud to have been joined on his journey by the Old One and his three young friends. The outcome showed that he had chosen the right course of action to take.

"Amy, you are the oldest in your family. My people would like you to tell them a story," David said. As he spoke, the village ladies quietly moved the children away from the group and busied them with a quiet activity that allowed them to listen while their hands were occupied.

"You are being honored. It is indeed a privilege and an honor to be asked to tell a story at a feast," Kadluk said.

"I don't know what to say. What story could I tell?" Amy asked, looking at Ty and Parker.

"I know, Amy. Tell them about your first pony ride. They'll love it," Parker said.

"Yeah, tell them that one." Ty started to laugh, remembering the occasion.

"You've got to tell them something. It might as well be the pony ride, unless you can think of something else," Parker said.

"Now that you've suggested the pony ride, I can't think of anything else," Amy replied as she stood up to the cheering of the villagers.

The events of Amy's first pony ride would be forever burned into her memory. She had only been three years old at the time of the visit to Uncle Newt's farm. She'd looked forward to the pony ride, but once on the little pony, he'd given her a stiff-legged trot that jarred her so badly she'd had to grab the saddle horn to keep from falling off.

Her audience had never seen a horse and didn't know what one was. They assumed Amy had been riding a wild caribou, and when she'd grabbed the saddle horn, they assumed she'd grabbed the caribou's antlers, which elicited a gasp of horror from the crowd. Being so young, her bravery made her stature grow in their eyes and they regaled her with laughter as she imitated the teeth-jarring ride the little pony had given her.

71

"You are a good storyteller. The villagers appreciate you sharing your story with them," David told Amy.

Shyly, the little kids approached Amy and presented her with a necklace they had made while listening to the stories.

"We want you to have this to remember us by and to thank you for your help in our rescue from Amayersuk," said Payton, the eldest of the little children.

"Why, thank you; it was an honor to be able to help," Amy replied as she took the necklace.

"Look, Amy! It has eight little kids carved from ivory hanging as charms from it!" Parker said.

"It's just beautiful. I will treasure it always," Amy remarked as she slipped the necklace around her neck.

"It is time to go," Kadluk said as he stood and walked towards his komatik.

"Already? Do we have to go so soon?" Ty asked.

"Yeah, I was just starting to really enjoy this," Parker added.

"There is much to do; we go now," Kadluk replied.

The villagers were clearly sad to see the kids and Kadluk depart. With the goodbyes said and everyone loaded on the komatik, the miles were soon exhausted as the dog team sped towards the tent covering the dig site.

Upon reaching the tent, Amy asked, *"Would you like tea and cookies before you leave, Old One?"*

"Yes, I would," he replied.

There's always food in the small kitchen in the tent where the emergency supplies are kept. Amy soon had the kettle boiling and before long Kadluk was enjoying boiling hot tea with the ample spoonfuls of sugar he so relished.

"Old One, how can this be?" Amy suddenly asked. *"It took five days to complete the journey to save the little kids, yet here we are and no time has passed."*

"What is time? You cannot feel it, it cannot feed you, and you cannot control it. It matters not. Do not concern yourself with things you have no control over," Kadluk informed her.

"Is it possible this never happened and we just dreamed it?" Amy asked.

"Do you think it was all a dream, Amy? Everything seemed so real," Ty remarked.

"What's that around your neck if you think this wasn't real? Where do you suppose you got that necklace?" Parker pointed at the little necklace that hung from Amy's neck.

Amy's right hand grasped the necklace and she knew right away this hadn't been a dream, because dreams don't make necklaces.

They heard the roar of skidoo engines that announced the arrival of Max and Bill at the dig site.

When the men entered the tent, they were glad to see Kadluk having tea with the kids. They shook hands and gestured their greetings by nodding their heads towards one another.

"Boy, I wish I could converse with this fellow," Max commented to Bill.

"I know what you mean. He could enlighten us on a lot of things about this site," Bill stated.

"Indeed he could, and it would probably save us a lot of digging to uncover what he already knows," Max stated.

"You know, Max, if I didn't know better, I would swear your kids and that old man can talk to each other," Bill said as he turned towards the dig and the work at hand.

"If only they could, Bill. If only they could," Max replied.

* * * the end * * *

GLOSSARY

Amayersuk - a giant woman who kidnaps errant children

Boogeyman - a frightening person, real or imaginary, used as a threat, especially towards children

Igloo - a small domed building made of snow blocks

Inua - (inh' oo ah) the spiritual occupants, or spirit helpers, that reside in all living or inanimate things

Inuit - (inh' oo it) the people

Inuk - an Inuit person

Ishigaq - a race of little people who live along the shoreline

Inukshuk - (stone figure) likeness of a person

Inyusuq - (personal souls) the powerful forces that reside within individuals and serve as the source of good health, stamina, willpower, and energy, all the elements that give a person life

Kabloona - white man

Kamik - (Mukluk or Amauti) an Inuit skin boot

Komatik - (koh-ma-tik) a sled with wooden runners and crossbars bound with animal hides

Nanook - polar bear

Sedna - a sea goddess who rules over all the lesser spirits and monsters, she is considered to be the mother of both land and sea creatures and therefore the provider of all life

Shaman - (Sham-man) a priest of shamanism, or a medicine man or witch doctor of a similar religion thought to have special abilities in relating to the supernatural

Tarrak - a dark, angry, and malicious spirit that becomes enraged when certain taboos are not adhered to by relatives after a person's death

Tundra - a vast treeless Arctic region with permanently frozen subsoil

Tutelary - (tew-till-lar-ee) having the role of guardian or protector, or of a guardian

The Author

Lawrence was born and raised in Alberta. 37 years of his adult life was spent serving in the Canadian Armed Forces and the Royal Canadian Mounted Police. The author draws on 10 years of living in the Yukon and the Northwest Territories for the inspiration for his stories. Retirement finds him again in Alberta where he presently lives with his wife Judith. They have 2 children and 6 grandchildren.

The Illustrator

Rob Adams, son of Lawrence Adams; when he is not working on his fathers illustrations, can be found working on game designs. Trained in Visual Communication, Rob currently works in the field of video games, juggling roles of a producer and game designer. Rob has had first hand experience of living and visiting many of the places described in the Trapps Family Adventure books.

Other books by Lawrence E.R. Adams.

The old one
The amulet
The stolen soul
The creator
The amulet
The mine

Watch for future books by Lawrence Adams as the Trapps Family Adventures continue to explore the mysteries of the north.

who walks on my land
who swims in my waters
who flies in my skies
The spirit of marble island
The search for the red diamond
The rescue

Join Amy, Ty and Parker as they continue to seek answers to life's adventures on the frozen tundra.

ACKNOWLEDGMENT

It is my sons artistic talent that gives meaning to the stories and helps bring them to life. Without him these stories would never have been written.